Harrietta's Hair

Written by
Mary Louise Zuccaro Pollock
Illustrated by
Heather Yatros-Barker

Mary Louise Zuccaro Pollock

ISBN #978-0-615-51086-6 (hardcover)
ISBN #978-0-615-51085-9 (softcover)

Illustrations by Heather Yatos Barker
Cover and Text design by Rose Island Bookworks

Tribute House Publishing
web site: www.tributehousepublishing.com
email: info@tributehousepublishing.com
phone: 810-496-2790

Manufactured by Color House Graphics, Inc.,
Grand Rapids, Michigan, USA
July 2011
Job# 35369-35370

To my grandchildren
Evan, Parker, Andrew, Kevin, Dennis, and
especially Mattison, the true Harrietta.
And, to all my former students.

Harrietta was a bright little girl with a beautiful smile that curved around her pearly white teeth. Big dimples appeared on her plump rosy cheeks when she giggled, which was often.

Harrietta was fun to have around.
She enjoyed riding her bicycle up
and down the sidewalk, was a whiz at
shooting baskets, and could run around
the bases quicker than any boy on her
baseball team.

Most people would say Harrietta was a perfect child, but there was one mystery about her. No one knew the color of her eyes. You see, Harrietta hated to brush her hair!!! Her golden locks would droop over her eyebrows like a waterfall covering her eyes. But no matter how many times people reminded her to brush her hair, Harrietta simply wouldn't listen.

"Brush your hair Harrietta," Mom would say as she got dressed for school. "Later," replied Harrietta. But alas, it would be time to leave for school and Harrietta still hadn't brushed her hair.

Harrietta loved to visit her grandmother.
They would have a jolly time baking cookies and playing games. But when Grandma told her to brush her hair so she could see her eyes, Harrietta replied, "I brushed it last week."

"What a stubborn child," Grandma would mutter under her breath.

Often Harrietta's cousins would stop over to play tag or walk through the fields looking for animal tracks.

"**W**hy don't you brush your hair so you can see where you are going?" they would ask. Harrietta just shrugged her shoulders and shouted, "Maybe I'll brush it tomorrow." The cousins simply laughed, as they found Harrietta to be quite amusing.

One summer evening Mom and Dad decided to take Harrietta camping. How she loved sleeping beneath the white moon and count stars as they twinkled above her.

Shortly after settling down inside her
cozy sleeping bag, Harrietta fell asleep.
Her knotted hair rested upon her fluffy
pillow.

As Harrietta slept peacefully, a mother opossum hanging by her tail on a tree limb noticed the tangled mass of hair below. "What a fine home this would make for my babies," she said aloud. So she gathered her babies and nestled right in.

A bit later, a young skunk sauntered by. "What a lovely place to take a nap," whispered the skunk when he spied the snarled curls upon Harrietta's pillow. Then quietly he snuggled in next to the sleeping opossum and her family.

Toward morning, a peppy chipmunk scurried about in search of a place to hide a few acorns. "This is the perfect hiding place," chattered the chipmunk as it stumbled upon Harrietta's messy curls. So three tiny acorns were tucked in next to the napping skunk.

When Harrietta awoke she wasn't
feeling quite right. Her head felt heavy
and it seemed to itch and tingle.
"Mom, Dad," called Harrietta.
"Come quick!"

"What's wrong Sweetie?" they asked. But when they looked at Harrietta they didn't need to wait for her answer.

Promptly they plucked out three acorns. Very gently they removed the napping skunk. Finally they coaxed the mother opossum to leave with her babies. "What a relief," sighed Harrietta.

Harrietta learned a valuable lesson
that morning. Ever since then, she has
brushed her hair every day
(sometimes twice).

Oh, by the way...

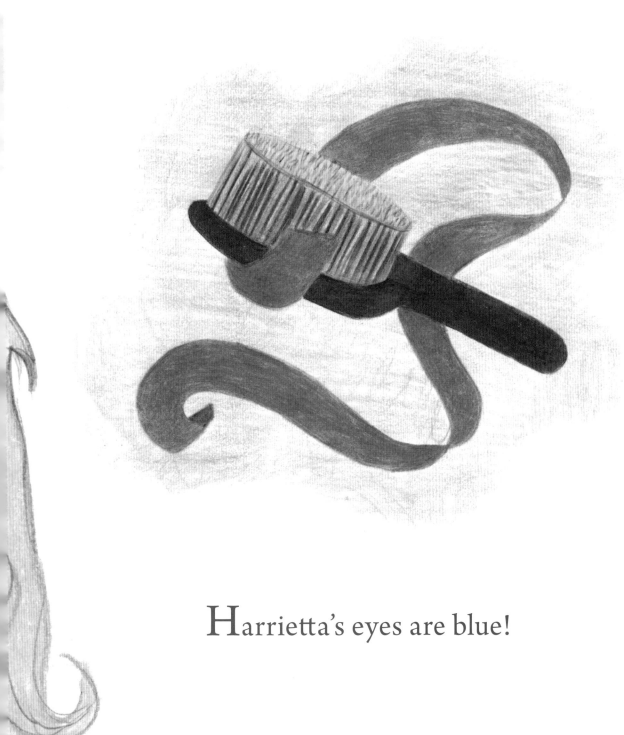

Harrietta's eyes are blue!

About the Author

Mary Louise grew up in Detroit, Michigan and is a graduate of Michigan State University. Though retired from teaching she continues to substitute teach in various St. Clair County schools. She and her husband, Dennis, live in Casco, Michigan. They have three grown children and six grandchildren. This is her first book.

Mary Louise acknowledges with gratitude her cousins Ron and Tom Zuccaro and Susan Leonard for guiding her through the publishing process.

About the Illustrator

Heather Yatros Barker grew up in Madison Heights, Michigan and presently lives in Sterling Heights, Michigan with her two sons, Richie and Tyler. She currently works for the Anchor Bay School District, and has been a freelance artist/muralist for years. Not only has she drawn many gifts for people, but she has also painted murals throughout Anchor Bay Schools and in many homes, including her own.

For Heather, the best part of designing a piece of artwork is the expression on a person's face when she is finished. She has been doodling, sketching, and drawing ever since she can remember. Other than being a mother, drawing is her passion. She is grateful for her gift, "ART."